Once a little bunny sat
in the dentist's chair.
He said, "My tooth is wiggly,
does it need repair?"
"No," said the dentist,
"Baby teeth fall out.
A new tooth has started growing,
surely without a doubt."

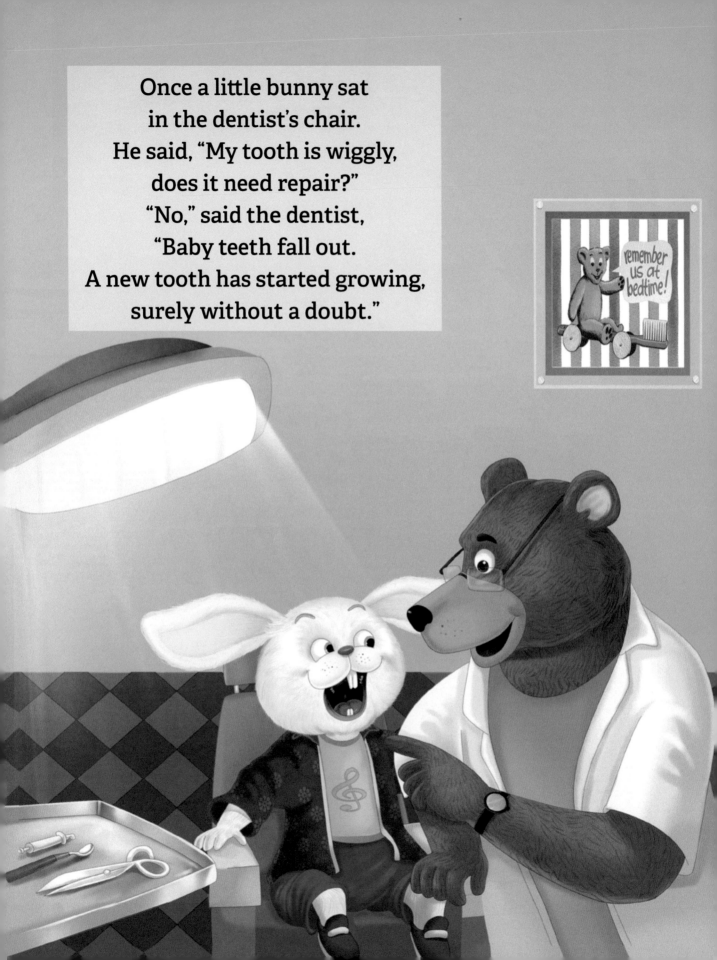

This book belongs to

_____

FOREVER FRIENDS CLUB

Published & Copyright © 2018 by Gaurav Bhatnagar
Forever Friends Books
www.foreverfriendsbooks.com

Illustrations by ePublishingeXperts Art Studio
www.epublishingexperts.com
Edited by Lor Bingham

This edition first published in 2018 by Gaurav Bhatnagar
All right reserved.

Ordering Information
Special discounts are available on quantity purchases by corporations, schools, libraries, charities, and others.

For information please email
foreverfriendsbooks@gmail.com
ISBN: 978-93-5346-048-8 (HB)
978-93-5346-172-0 (PB)

Printed in India
First printing , 2018

Dedication Page

Dedicated to my parents
For their love, endless support, encouragement & sacrifices

And to my wife Arti
Thank you for being my best friend, a perfect homemaker,
a lovely mother, and a successful teacher.
Thanks for everything.

A special thanks to my son, Krishant
My best stress buster and the inspiration to write this story.

- Gaurav

This news upset the bunny;
he was proud of his front teeth.
He asked, "Can they be saved?"
I don't want more underneath.
The mother's words were helpful,
simple yet quite wise,
"Your grown-up teeth are stronger,
and they're of a different size."

One day he moved his tongue
to give his tooth a jiggle.
But looking in the mirror just
made him smile and giggle.
"Mommy," he yelled, "my tooth
is gone, and I am very glad!"
But bunny's brother laughed
at him, and he felt really sad.

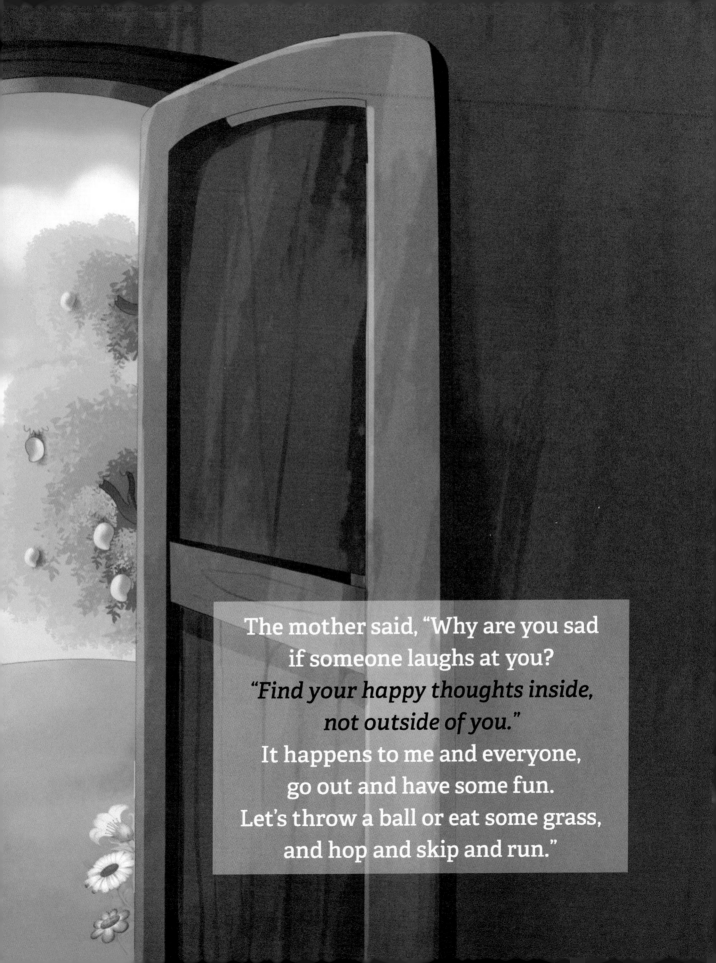

The mother said, "Why are you sad
if someone laughs at you?
"*Find your happy thoughts inside,
not outside of you.*"
It happens to me and everyone,
go out and have some fun.
Let's throw a ball or eat some grass,
and hop and skip and run."

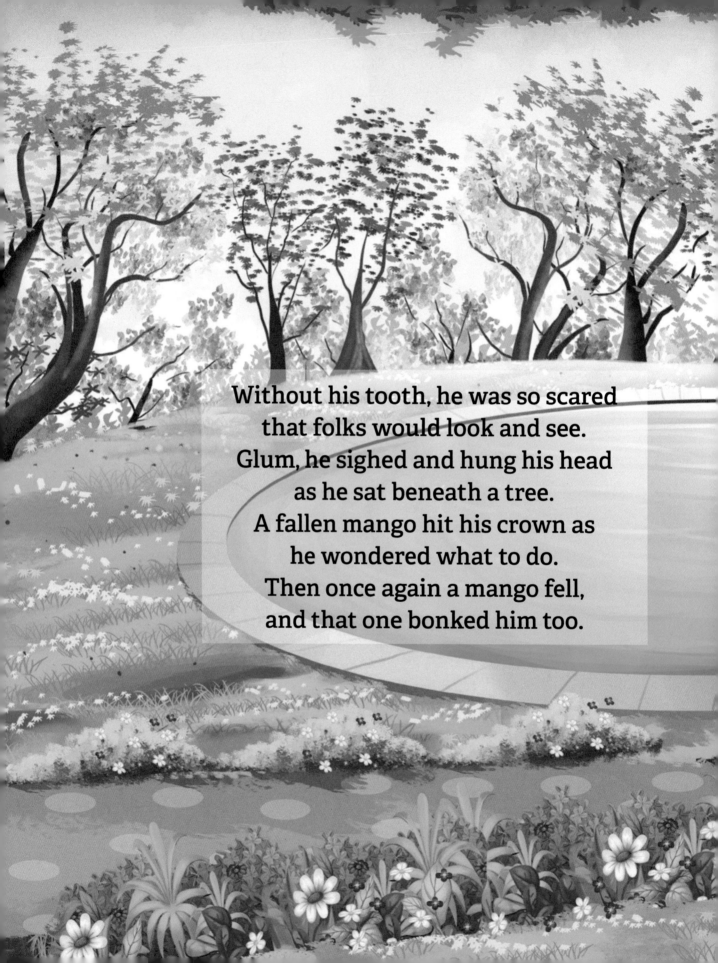

Without his tooth, he was so scared
that folks would look and see.
Glum, he sighed and hung his head
as he sat beneath a tree.
A fallen mango hit his crown as
he wondered what to do.
Then once again a mango fell,
and that one bonked him too.

"Who is it?" yelled the bunny;
he looked up in the tree,
"Who's up there dancing in the leaves,
throwing mangoes down on me?"
A naughty little monkey sat laughing in the leaves.
"Is it still you the cheeky monkey who wants to pester me?"

Instead of getting angry
the bunny hatched a plan,
I won't get mad, I won't be sad;
I'll make friends if I can.
"Please," he said politely,
"come down and talk with me.
"It's difficult to make new friends
if you hide in a tree."

The cheeky monkey grabbed some leaves
from tree limbs beneath.
The bunny was amazed to see
he too had missing teeth!
No longer did he feel alone
his friend was toothless but still cheery,
Perhaps they two could start a club to make
the days less dreary?

The bunny and the monkey put
posters on some trees.
*"If you have lost a baby tooth
then come and join us, please!"*
Spike the hedgehog saw the sign
while digging in the shrub,
"My tooth is wiggly as can be;
may I please join your club?"

Next to join was Frisky Squirrel,
living in a tree.
Right behind him, Funny Giraffe
stretching his neck to see.

They made a sign and raised it,
for their message to be seen.
Way high atop a post,
in letters large and green.

"Let's have some fun," said Funny Giraffe.
"Maybe picnic by the pool?"
"I'll bring a camera," the bunny said.
"We'll swim to keep us cool."
"Some yummy food," said Cheeky Monkey,
"Mangoes from the tree,"
"Umm... Let's eat worms," another said,
"Oh please, no worms for me!"

The newfound friends enjoyed themselves.
They swam, and danced, and jumped.
Till Hedgehog cried," Oh my! It seems
I've just been bumped!"

It was a Baby Elephant;
whose ears were huge and pink.
He said, "I've lost my tooth,
so I can only drink."

The Baby Elephant was glad,
he splashed and pranced around.
He jumped and played with his new friends,
in the club that he had found.

Drowsy Sloth crawled slowly there;
it took most of the day.
But he was keen to join the fun,
to have some friends and play.

They welcomed Sloth except the
Squirrel, who was playing in the pool.
All full of verve he thought the
Sloth was very far from cool.
But then he saw the Sloth had skills,
he was showing them, Kung Fu.
He'd been wrong to judge the Sloth
and cheered a loud **"Yahoo!"**

Taking turns and photos, "Say **CHEESE**,"
they yelled, "and **SMILE!**"
The friends made funny faces and
laughed for quite awhile.

"To lose our baby teeth is fine,
it happens," said the bunny,
"When your friends are different too,
you don't feel sad or funny!"

The friends laughed hard and
played in groups until the sky grew dark.
They promised they would meet again
the next day in the park.
They left the sign high on
the post for everyone to see.
Because *"Forever Friends Club"*
was the funniest place to be.

Let's Talk About It..

1. **The bunny was sad because his brother laughed at him.** Do you think if someone talks bad about you or laugh at you will make you sad? How will you react in that situation?

2. **The cheeky monkey threw mangoes on the bunny, but he decided to be polite and friendly instead of becoming angry.** Do you think being polite and friendly can diffuse an otherwise heated and violent situation?

3. **The bunny and monkey invited other characters in the story to be a part of their club by putting posters and banners.** What if you form a "Forever Friends Club", how will you invite and make new friends?

4. **The squirrel judged the drowsy sloth too early without knowing him personally.** Do you think it's good to know a person first before judging him or her?

5. What is that thing you love most to do in company with your friends?

Email me your thoughts and what is the best part of the story that you liked. My email id is foreverfriendsbooks@gmail.com.

And if you enjoyed the story, post an honest review at Amazon.

Made in the USA
San Bernardino,
CA